me
Blossom

Gran

Nan

for Luke, Rosie, Carl and Paul - with love
B.A.

for Myrthlyn
C.T.

ORCHARD BOOKS
96 Leonard Street, London EC2A 4XD
Orchard Books Australia
32/45-51 Huntley Street, Alexandria, NSW 2015
ISBN 1 84121 625 9 (hardback)
ISBN 1 84121 278 4 (paperback)
First published in Great Britain in 2002
First paperback publication in 2003
Text © Bernard Ashley 2002
Illustrations © Carol Thompson 2002
The right of Bernard Ashley to be identified as the author and of
Carol Thompson to be identified as the illustrator of this work has been asserted
by them in accordance with the Copyright, Designs and Patents Act, 1988.
A CIP catalogue record for this book is available from the British Library.
1 3 5 7 9 10 8 6 4 2 (hardback)
5 7 9 10 8 6 4 (paperback)
Printed in China

DOUBLE

the
LOVE

Written by Bernard Ashley

Illustrated by Carol Thompson

ORCHARD BOOKS

Blossom was a lucky girl.
She had two grandmothers.
The city one she called 'Nan'.
The country one she
called 'Gran'.

Nan

Gran

Blossom lived in the city so she saw Nan a lot.
She looked after Blossom when her mum was up to something busy.
Blossom and Nan had lots of special sayings,
and they did special things.

"Come on, Nan," said Blossom. "Let's do a Tinga Layo!"

"Tinga layo! Me donkey buck, me donkey leap, me donkey kick with his two hind feet," said Nan.

And she would give Blossom a bouncy ride on her back.

Nan often took Blossom to the park and they danced
along hand in hand through the trees.
And when they got home Nan would give Blossom lemonade
and her favourite gingerbread biscuits.

Blossom saw Gran in the holidays.
They all went to stay in her little house. Mum and Dad
squeezed into the spare room with Blossom on the folding bed.
Blossom and Gran had lots of special sayings,
and they did special things.

"Love-a-duck!
Cluck! Cluck!"
said Blossom.

And Gran would take Blossom down to
the farm to see the ducks and the hens.

And they often had a picnic in the field behind the house.
Gran brought Blossom apple juice
and her favourite cheesy biscuits.
Then Blossom would say,
"Come on, Gran. Let's play ring-a-ring-a-roses!"
And they swung around and all fell down in a heap laughing.

When they were back in the
city, Gran telephoned every
Sunday and spoke to Blossom.
She made her voice sound very close.

City Nan and Country Gran.
Blossom loved them both.

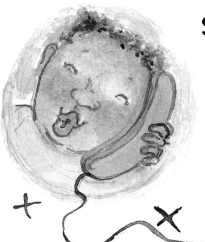

Then Blossom's new little brother was born, and there was a party. It was at Blossom's own city house, and everyone came - even Gran, all that way! It was the first time Blossom had ever seen Nan and Gran together! What fun!

But Nan didn't rush to get Blossom any lemonade.
And Gran didn't fetch Blossom any apple juice.

They both stayed sitting
down and kept themselves quiet...

...until Blossom fell over.

She bumped her forehead and it knocked
her breath out. It made her cry.
Quick as a flash, Nan was there and Gran
was there. They cuddled Blossom between
them in a Nan-and-Gran sandwich.
Blossom got a city kiss on one cheek and
a country kiss on the other.

Blossom kept hold of both their
hands, and wouldn't let go.
"Come on," said Blossom, pulling.
"Where?" asked Nan and Gran.
"In the other room.
Let's have some fun!"
said Blossom.

Nan put on a tape.
"Gran - do you know the steps of this dance?" she asked.
And Gran did some fancy steps and twists.

Nan and Gran and Blossom
danced, all three of
them together.

Suddenly the music played an old song.
Both Gran and Nan joined in.
Then Nan scooped up Blossom on to Gran's back.
"Tinga layo!" said Blossom, and they trotted off,
in and out of the kitchen, up and
down the passage, tinga-layo-ing,
singing and bouncing.

Then, "Ring-a-ring-a-roses!" said Blossom. Everyone made a circle and got mixed up together when 'bump!' they all fell down, laughing and clapping.

"You've got to bring yourself
to the city for a visit,"
Nan said to Gran.
"And you've got to come to
the country for a holiday!"
Gran said to Nan.
Blossom didn't know
she could feel so happy.
When her two grandmothers
get together, she has
double the fun
and also...

double the love.

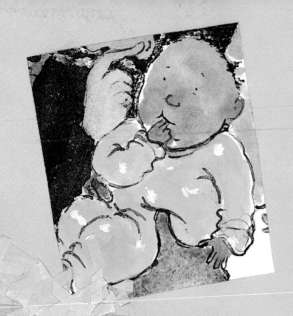

my
new
brother

Friday 15th

Gran
visits
Nan

Nan visits
Gran
June 1st – 4th

Dad
Mum
Nan and
Gran and
baby and
me